This WALKER book belongs to:

_____

_____

For River, who makes everything feel
brand new. R. B.

For Renate and Wilhelm
And with special thanks to my dear Julius, who
helped with creating the hand lettering. Y. R.

First published 2016 by Walker Books Ltd
87 Vauxhall Walk, London SE11 5HJ

10 9 8 7 6 5 4 3 2 1

Text © 2016 Rachel Bright Illustrations © 2016 Yu Rong

The right of Rachel Bright and Yu Rong to be identified
as author and illustrator respectively of this work
has been asserted by them in accordance with
the Copyright, Designs and Patents Act 1988

This book has been typeset in Jacoby Light Condensed

Printed in China

British Library Cataloguing in Publication Data:
a catalogue record for this book is available from
the British Library.

ISBN 978-1-4063-7181-9

www.walker.co.uk

Snowflake iN My Pocket

Rachel Bright   illustrated by Yu Rong

WALKER BOOKS
AND SUBSIDIARIES
LONDON · BOSTON · SYDNEY · AUCKLAND

Once upon a winter,
in a faraway place, the last few leaves
of an old, twisted oak tree rattled in the breeze.

Inside that oak tree, lived a very wise bear
and a very small squirrel.
Bear had seen a hundred seasons, maybe more.
And Squirrel? Well, he had only seen three.

Together they
explored the four corners
of the forest. And whatever
Bear did, Squirrel tried, too.

wooo-hooo!
splosh-splish!

Munch-munch!

Wherever they went,
Bear had always
been there before.
But somehow
it all felt brand
new again with
Squirrel by his side.

One icy night,
as their breath blew in clouds,
Bear whispered, "It's on its way."
"*What is?*" sniffed Squirrel.

"Oh..." Bear puffed. "The snow."
Squirrel gasped. "Will it snow *tonight*?
Do you think that it *might*?"

But a bear can never be *exactly* sure when
the weather will change. He just knows that it will.

So Squirrel tried his very hardest to stay awake
ALL NIGHT, searching and searching the twinkling sky.
But sometime between one star and the next,

he accidentally drifted off into a flurry of dreams.

So when the morning shone through his window,
he woke with a fast-beating heart, *thumpety-thud.*

With a *squeak-squeeeedge*, he cleared a hole
in the frost to see and ...

oh!

There was *MAGIC* surrounding their tree!

The snow *had* come in the night,
but ... so had the sniffles for Bear!

A...A...A...CHOOO!

And a bear with the sniffles
must stay in his bed until he is better.

So Squirrel tucked him up, took a deep breath
and promised to have fun for both of them.

Crunch ...

crunch...

Squirrel's footsteps were the only sound in the forest.

Crunch ... crunch ... crumbletycrunchCRUNCHCRUNCHCRUNCH!

He ran
and rolled!

He made snow angels ...

and snow bears!

It was the most *perfect* morning.

Well, *almost* perfect.
For nothing could be completely perfect
without Bear.

In the silvery stillness,
a wonderful thought
tumbled into
Squirrel's head...

"I

could

CATCH

a snowflake ...

and take it home to Bear!"

He ran in happy circles,

as they fell,

catching the snowflakes

until

he found

the *perfectest* one.

Then he put it in his pocket and set off for home.

"Bear!" he called. "Are you there? You couldn't come to the snow, so I've brought the snow to you!" And he reached in his pocket...

But where his snowflake used to be ...

there was
nothing
at all.

"Where has it
gone?" Squirrel
said, as Bear
took his paw.

"Snow comes and snow goes," Bear said,

"but ONE thing lasts forever."

And as they cuddled up by the fire, which crackled

and popped and kept their toes warm,

Squirrel said, "Me and you?"

"Now and always," whispered Bear.

Rachel Bright has written and illustrated several books for children, including *Love Monster* and *My Sister is an Alien*, and is the author of *The Lion Inside*, illustrated by Jim Field. She is also the creator of the award-winning stationery and homeware range, The Bright Side. Rachel lives on a farm near the seaside with her partner, their daughter, a dog called Elvis and a cat called Superman.

About this book she says, "May every snowflake be a reminder to reach for the wonderfulness in life, without holding on too tight, since the things we can treasure for always, aren't really things at all."

Find Rachel online at www.lookonthebrightside.co.uk and on twitter as @Rachel_Bright2

Yu Rong, author and illustrator of *A Lovely Day for Amelia Goose* and illustrator of *Tracks of a Panda*, was born and raised in China. She studied at the Royal College of Art.

Inspired by happy memories from her childhood, Yu Rong likes to bring traditional Chinese art forms – such as the papercut artwork of *A Snowflake in My Pocket* – to the picture book page. "Snowflakes bring out the love in Squirrel and Bear's simple, warm life. Even the coldest, most frozen things can be transformed into the warmest, most cherished love which Bear and Squirrel share," she says.

Yu Rong works and lives in Cambridge with her husband, three children and their dog Captain Sniff.

Find her online at www.yurong.co.uk